Science Fair Flop

Ready, Freddy!

Ready, Freddy!

Science Fair Flop

by ABBY KLEIN

illustrated by
JOHN MCKINLEY

Scholastic Inc.
New York Toronto London Auckland
Sydney Mexico City New Delhi Hong Kong

To Anne—
A gifted teacher who knew how to open
children's eyes to the world around them.
You will always be in my heart!
—A.K.

ISBN 978-0-545-13048-6

12 11 10 9 8 7 6   12 13 14 15/0

Printed in the U.S.A.   40
First printing, December 2010

CHAPTERS

I have a problem.

A really, really big problem.

Every year my school has a science fair. Last year, when I was in kindergarten, I could share a collection, so I showed my shark tooth collection. Now that I am in first grade, I have to do an experiment for the fair, but I can't think of any good projects.

Let me tell you about it.

CHAPTER 1

What Is a Hypothesis?

"Come to the rug, everybody," said my teacher, Mrs. Wushy. "I want to show you an experiment."

"I love experiments!" said my best friend, Robbie.

"If you love them so much, then maybe you should marry them," Max said, laughing.

"You can't marry an experiment!" said Chloe.

"Yes, you can," Max said with a grin.

"Oh, no, you can't!"

"Yes, you can."

"Max, Chloe, that is enough," said Mrs. Wushy. "I need to have everybody's eyes looking at me now."

Max and Chloe glared at each other and then turned to look at Mrs. Wushy.

"When scientists do an experiment, they have a question they want to answer. With this question in mind, they make a hypothesis. Does anyone know what that means?" asked Mrs. Wushy.

Robbie's hand shot up. "I know! I know!" he said.

When it comes to science, Robbie knows everything. He is a science genius.

"Yes, Robbie," said Mrs. Wushy. "Tell the class what a hypothesis is."

"When a scientist makes a hypothesis, he is predicting what he thinks is going to happen in the experiment."

"You're such a brain," said Max. "I don't know what you just said."

"It's like a guess," said Robbie. "The scientist is guessing what he thinks is going to happen when he does the experiment."

"That's right!" said Mrs. Wushy. "And today

we are all going to be scientists. Each of you will get a chance to make a hypothesis."

"Cool," said my friend Jessie. "Science is fun!"

"What is the experiment going to be about?" asked Robbie.

"We are going to do a float-and-sink experiment," said Mrs. Wushy. "Can anyone think of something that floats?"

"A rubber duckie!" Max shouted out.

"I bet he plays with one of those when he takes a bath," I whispered to Robbie.

We both laughed.

"Anything else?"

"A plastic cup," said Chloe. "I like to pretend I'm cooking when I take a bath, so I have lots of plastic cups and bowls in the tub, and they all float."

"What do you cook?" asked Max. "Fried worms?"

"Eeeeewwwwww! That's disgusting," said

Chloe, wrinkling up her nose. "I would never make fried worms. I'd make beautiful cherry pies, and cupcakes with pink frosting."

"Too bad they're not real," Jessie whispered to me. "That sounds yummy!"

My stomach growled. "Did you hear that?" I whispered to Jessie. "My stomach is yelling, 'CUPCAKE! CUPCAKE!'"

"Those are great answers so far," said Mrs. Wushy. "Anything else?"

"Well, once I was trying to write something down while I was taking a bath," said Robbie, "and my pencil fell in the tub. When I looked down, it was floating on top of the water."

"Only you would be writing in the bathtub!" I whispered.

Robbie smiled.

"Good," said Mrs. Wushy. "Now let's see if you can think of some things that sink."

"A rock!" Max shouted out.

"Max, please remember to raise your hand if

you have something to say," said Mrs. Wushy. "It isn't okay to shout out."

Jessie raised her hand.

"Thank you for raising your hand, Jessie," said Mrs. Wushy. "Do you have an idea?"

"Yes," said Jessie. "A penny. I know a penny sinks, because my mom throws them in the pool for me, and then I dive down and get them."

"Hey, I do that, too!" I said. "I love that game!"

Lots of other kids said, "Me, too! Me, too!"

"How about one more?" asked Mrs. Wushy. "Do you have an idea, Freddy?"

"Ummm . . . ummm . . . a shoe. One time I was in a boat with my dad. We were fishing, and I was swinging my legs over the side of the boat. Then all of a sudden my shoe went flying off and fell in the water. It sank to the bottom of the lake, and I never saw it again."

"Max, please put the pumpkin down and go back to your spot," said Mrs. Wushy.

Kids started shouting, "Sink! Sink! Sink!"

"Okay, everyone, quiet down," said Mrs. Wushy. "You will all get to make a hypothesis. You will make your own guess about what will happen when we put the pumpkin in this bucket of water."

"I know I'm right," Max said. "It's going to sink for sure."

"Please write your name on this little piece of paper, and then stick it on this chart," Mrs. Wushy said, passing out slips of paper. "Put it on the 'float' side if you think the pumpkin will float, or on the 'sink' side if you think it will sink."

I wrote my name on my piece of paper, but then I just sat there and stared at it.

"Come on, Freddy," said Jessie. "You have to put your paper up on the chart."

"I know," I said. "I just don't know what to do. I think it's going to sink, but Robbie thinks it's going to float, and he is always right." I raised my hand.

"Yes, Freddy," said Mrs. Wushy.

"What if our guess isn't right?"

"That's okay," said Mrs. Wushy. "Scientists do

lots of experiments. Sometimes their hypothesis is right, and sometimes it is wrong."

I walked up to the chart and stuck my name on the "sink" side. Robbie was my best friend, but there was no way a pumpkin was going to float.

CHAPTER 2

The Experiment

Mrs. Wushy looked at the chart. "It looks like everybody thinks the pumpkin will sink except for Robbie."

Max started pointing at Robbie and laughing. "Ha, ha, ha, ha! He thinks it's going to float. Ha, ha, ha!"

"Max, that is not okay," said Mrs. Wushy. "We do not laugh at our friends like that. Do you want to be here for the experiment?"

Max nodded.

"Then you need to sit down and be quiet."

Max quickly sat down.

"So far we have done two important things," said Mrs. Wushy. "We've asked a question, and we've made a hypothesis. Next we have to make sure we have the materials we will need for this experiment."

"What kind of materials?" Chloe asked. "Velvet? Silk?"

"No," Mrs. Wushy said with a smile. "Not that kind of material, Chloe. I just meant the things we need to do the experiment. What do we need?"

"A pumpkin!" I said.

"A bucket and some water!" Jessie said.

"Good," said Mrs. Wushy. "I have all of those things, so I think we are ready to do the experiment. Is everyone ready?"

"Ready!" we all said.

Mrs. Wushy lifted the pumpkin and gently placed it into the bucket of water.

I held my breath.

"Sink! Sink! Sink!" some kids chanted.

All of a sudden, the room got quiet.

We all stared at the bucket.

We couldn't believe our eyes! That big, fat pumpkin was floating on top of the water, happily bobbing up and down.

I looked at Max. His eyes were wide, and his mouth was hanging open.

Then I looked at Robbie. He sat there with a huge smile on his face.

"I can't believe it," Jessie whispered.

"I can't, either," I said.

"When a scientist does an experiment, he or she must collect data," said Mrs. Wushy. "That means the scientist has to write down what is happening during the experiment. What do you see happening?"

"The pumpkin is floating," said Chloe.

"That's just because you didn't push it down," said Max. "You have to push it down in the bucket, and then it will sink."

"Max, do you want to try pushing it down?" asked Mrs. Wushy.

"Yes," said Max.

"Well, then come up here and give it a push. Just don't push too hard, because I don't want the water to spill on the carpet."

Max walked up with a smile and gave the pumpkin a big push. "Now it will sink," he said. He turned around and walked back to his spot.

Everyone started laughing.

"What's so funny?" asked Max.

"See for yourself," Chloe said.

Max looked at the bucket, and the pumpkin was once again floating on top of the water.

"That's just crazy," said Max, shaking his head.

Mrs. Wushy smiled. "Does anyone know why the pumpkin floats?"

Of course Robbie raised his hand. "Because it's full of air," he said. "Things that have a lot of air in them float."

"That's right," said Mrs. Wushy. "Has anyone ever cut open a pumpkin?"

Lots of kids raised their hands.

"What's inside?"

"Ooey, gooey, disgusting goop that I won't touch!" said Chloe.

"You mean the pumpkin pulp," said Robbie.

"I don't know what it's called," said Chloe. "I just know it's slimy and disgusting."

"What else is in the pumpkin?" asked Mrs. Wushy.

"Lots and lots of seeds," said Jessie. "I love to toast them and eat them."

"Me, too! Me, too!" everyone said.

"Is the inside of the pumpkin solid?" asked Mrs. Wushy. "What about the inside of a watermelon? If I cut off the top of a watermelon, could I stick my hand inside?"

"No!" said Max.

"But I can stick my hand inside the pumpkin," said Mrs. Wushy, "because the pumpkin is full of air. Just like Robbie told us. If something has a lot of air inside it, then it will float."

"Hey! The raft in my pool is full of air, and it floats," said Chloe. "I like to lie on it in my swimsuit and float around, so my beautiful curls don't get wet."

"Is she for real?" Jessie asked.

"So now let's review what we have done so far," said Mrs. Wushy. "We asked a question, we made a hypothesis, we got our materials, and we did the experiment and collected our data. We just have one thing left."

"What's that?" Jessie asked.

"We have to write down our results. We have to say what happened."

"The pumpkin floated," I said.

"That's right. We can write that down right here on our chart," said Mrs. Wushy. "Now you all know the important steps to doing an experiment."

"Can we do another one?" Jessie asked.

"Another one! Another one!" we all chanted.

"I'm sorry, boys and girls. We don't have time to do another one today. But the good news is the science fair is coming up. Each of you will be doing an experiment for the science fair."

"Cool," said Max.

"When is the science fair?" asked Jessie.

"It is three weeks away," said Mrs. Wushy.

"Three weeks away?" said Chloe. "Then why are you telling us about it now?"

"Because to do a project for the fair, you need time to think of your experiment, and then you need time to do it. Some experiments may take a few weeks."

"A few weeks?" asked Jessie. "What do you mean?"

"Well, for example, say you wanted to do an experiment about how plants grow. Do plants grow overnight?" asked Mrs. Wushy.

"No!" Jessie said, laughing.

"So you might have to wait a few weeks to see the results of your experiment," said Mrs. Wushy.

"Oh, I get it," said Jessie.

"You should all start thinking about what you want to do," said Mrs. Wushy.

"I already know what I want to do," said Robbie.

"Of course you do," I thought. I, on the other hand, had no idea!

CHAPTER 3

Mice, Worms, and Nail Polish

When we got to the cafeteria for lunch, all the kids were talking about their ideas for their experiments. Everyone except me.

"Robbie, you said you already know what you want to do. What's your idea?" asked Jessie.

"Well, you know my mouse, Cheesy?"

"You mean the one that got loose one time in Freddy's house and totally freaked his mom out?"

Robbie looked at me, and I looked at him, and we both started laughing. Some of my milk almost came out of my nose.

"Yeah, that one," Robbie said.

"A mouse?" said Chloe. "You have a mouse for a pet?"

"Yeah," said Robbie. "He's so cute."

"Cute!" said Chloe. "Mice are not cute. They are stinky and gross."

"No, *you* are stinky and gross," said Max.

"I am not!" Chloe yelled. "You take that back, Max Sellars."

Max held his nose and sang, "Stinky, stinky, stinky, gross, gross, gross."

Chloe got so mad her face turned as red as her hair. I thought steam might start coming out of her ears.

"Just ignore him," said Jessie. "I want to hear what Robbie is going to do with Cheesy."

"I'm going to build a little maze for Cheesy. Then I'm going to put a piece of food at the

end of the maze, so Cheesy will want to run through the maze to get the food. Each time he runs, I'll time him to see how fast he goes. I'm going to put different kinds of food at the end of the maze and see if he runs faster depending on what food is there."

"Wow! That sounds pretty complicated," said Jessie.

"Not for Robbie," I said. "He is the science king!"

Robbie smiled. "How about you, Jessie? What do you want to do for your experiment?"

"I'm not totally sure yet. But I think I want to do something with jalapeños."

"Hal . . . a . . . whats?" I said.

"Jalapeños," said Jessie. "They are really hot peppers that are used a lot in Mexican food."

"Oh, I eat those all the time," said Max. "They're not that hot."

"You do not," said Jessie. "They're so hot that you would not even be able to eat one without crying like a baby."

I laughed just thinking about Max crying like a baby.

"I can bring one to school tomorrow, and you can eat it in front of all of us at lunchtime."

"Uh . . . that's okay," Max mumbled as he took a bite of his sandwich.

"Anyway," said Jessie, "my *abuela,* my grandma, grows them in a little box on the windowsill in our apartment."

"Why does she have them on the windowsill?" I asked.

"Because she says they need lots of sunlight to grow."

"I got it!" said Robbie. "Why don't you put some jalapeño plants in the sun, and put some other ones in your closet in the dark, and then see which ones grow better? That way you can prove whether or not they really need a lot of sun to grow."

"That's a great idea! Thanks, Robbie," said Jessie. "I'm going to try that experiment."

"What about me?" Chloe whined.

"What about her?" I whispered to Robbie.

"Does anyone want to hear what I'm going to do for the science fair?"

"Do we have a choice?" Jessie whispered to me.

"I'm going to do an experiment with nail polish."

"Nail polish?" said Max. "That sounds really dumb."

"You aren't allowed to say that word, Max," said Chloe.

Max stuck his tongue out at her.

Chloe turned back to us.

"What's your experiment?" asked Robbie.

"My friend Sabrina uses one kind of nail polish, and I use a different kind. She always says that hers is better, and I always say that mine is better."

"Who's Sabrina?" Jessie whispered.

I shrugged. "Maybe it's her imaginary friend."

Jessie giggled.

Chloe continued, "I'm going to paint the nails on one of my hands with Sabrina's kind of nail polish and the nails on my other hand with my kind of nail polish. Then I'm going to see which one chips off first."

"That's a good idea," said Robbie.

"Thank you," Chloe said, smiling.

"My experiment is going to be way better than that!" said Max.

"Really?" asked Jessie. "What's your experiment?"

"It's a worm experiment," said Max.

"Worms? Eeeeeeeewwwwwwwww," said Chloe.

"Worms are not eeeeewwwwww," said Max. "They're slimy and cool."

"Why do you always have to talk about such disgusting things?" Chloe asked. "You're making me sick." She grabbed her stomach and stuck out her tongue.

"If you think I'm so gross, then why don't you do us all a favor and go sit somewhere else?" asked Max.

"I think I will," said Chloe. She picked up her lunch box and went to sit at another table.

"So, what is your experiment?" Robbie asked Max.

"People say that if a worm gets cut in half, it grows back the other half it lost."

"Really?" I said.

"Yeah," said Max. "Cool, huh?"

I had never heard that before. It *was* kind of cool.

"So to prove that, I'm going to get a bunch

of worms, cut them in half, and see if they grow back into whole worms again."

"Only *you* would think of an experiment like that," said Jessie, shaking her head.

"I know. It's awesome," said Max.

Jessie turned to me and said, "So, Freddy, what about you?"

"What about me?"

"What experiment are you going to do?"

I shook my head. "I don't know."

"What do you mean you don't know?" Robbie asked.

Was I not speaking English? "I mean I have no idea what I'm going to do for the science fair."

And that was the truth. All the other kids knew exactly what they were going to do, but I had no idea. My mind was completely blank!

CHAPTER 4

Nothing!

That night, at dinner, Suzie had to bring up the science fair. "Guess what?" she asked.

"What?" said my mother.

"The science fair is coming up soon."

"Oh my goodness! I forgot all about the science fair," said my mom. "When is it? Do you still have time to do an experiment?"

"Don't worry, Mom," Suzie said. "The fair isn't for another three weeks. Our teachers just gave us the forms to fill out today."

"So what are you going to do this year?" my dad asked.

"I'm trying to decide. I have a few different ideas," Suzie said.

"Of course you do," I mumbled.

"What did you say, Freddy?" my mom asked.

"Nothing," I said, stuffing a forkful of broccoli into my mouth.

"Freddy, please take smaller bites. You're trying to shove a lot of food into a little mouth."

Suzie snickered. "A little mouth. I don't think Freddy has a little mouth."

"You don't?" asked my mom.

"No. He has a big mouth. A really big mouth."

"I do not!" I yelled at her, with my mouth full of broccoli.

"Freddy, do not talk with your mouth full," said my mom. "It isn't polite."

"But I don't have a big mouth. She does," I said, pointing to Suzie.

As I spoke, a small piece of broccoli flew out of my mouth and landed on Suzie's shirt.

Suzie jumped up from the table and started dancing around. "Eeewwwww! Eeewwwww! He spit on me! He spit on me!"

"Calm down, Suzie," said my mom. "I'll get a sponge and wipe it off. Follow me to the sink."

"Freddy," said my dad, "you stay here and finish chewing your food."

"Hurry up, Mom! It's so gross," said Suzie, shaking her hands in the air. "I want it off!"

My mom grabbed a sponge and wiped the little bit of broccoli off Suzie's shirt. "There. All better," she said. "Now come back to the table and sit down."

"Are you kidding?" said Suzie. "I can't come

41

back to the table until I change my shirt. I can't sit in a shirt that he spit on!"

"But I wiped it off," said my mom.

"It still has his saliva and cooties all over it," said Suzie.

"Fine. Go change," said my dad, "and then come back and tell us your ideas for the science fair. I can't wait to hear them."

"Can't wait," I thought.

Suzie ran upstairs and my parents turned to me. "Freddy, how many times have we told you not to talk with your mouth full of food?" said my mom.

"A lot," I whispered.

"When Suzie comes back down, you need to tell her you're sorry," said my dad.

I nodded.

Just then Suzie raced into the kitchen wearing her raincoat.

"Why do you have your raincoat on?" my mom asked.

"Just in case some more food comes flying at me. I'll be protected."

"I don't think you have to worry about that anymore," my mom said. "Right, Freddy?"

I nodded.

"Freddy has something to say to you," said my dad.

"Sorry," I whispered.

"What was that? I didn't hear you," said Suzie.

"Sorry!" I said a little more loudly.

"Now why don't you tell us all about your ideas for the science fair?" my mom said.

"Well, you know I like cooking, right?"

"Right," said my mom.

"So I was thinking I could do an experiment that had to do with cooking," said Suzie.

"That's a good idea," said my dad.

"I had two ideas about cooking," said Suzie.

"What's the first one?" my mom asked.

"Well, you know how I like making Popsicles with fruit juice? I thought I could make Popsicles with different kinds of fruit juice, like apple juice, orange juice, and grape juice."

"That's not an experiment," I said.

"I would keep track of what order the juice froze in. For my experiment, I would be asking the question, which fruit juice freezes the quickest?"

44

"I like that idea," said my dad. "What is the other one?"

"I love baking cookies, but I always wondered what the baking soda was for. I thought that I could make one batch of cookies with baking soda and one without baking soda. Then I could compare the two batches. My question would .be, why is baking soda so important when making cookies?"

"That's another great idea," said my mom.

"Thanks," Suzie said, smiling.

"Which one are you going to do?" asked my dad.

"I don't know. It's so hard to choose."

I put my head in my hands and let out a big sigh. Suzie had two great ideas, and I had nothing.

"What about you, Freddy?" asked my mom.

At first I didn't even look up.

"Freddy, your mother is talking to you," my dad said.

I slowly lifted my head out of my hands and looked around the table at my family. Then I jumped out of my chair and yelled, "I have nothing! Everyone has ideas for the science fair except me! I don't have one single idea. I have a big, fat nothing! Zip . . . zilch . . . zero!"

CHAPTER 5

Fuzzy Green Stuff

The next day I went over to Robbie's house to help him set up the maze for his experiment with Cheesy. He said that while we were working on his experiment, maybe he could help me think of something to do.

"I got this big cardboard box," said Robbie. "I was thinking I could build the maze in this."

"How are you going to do that?" I asked.

"Well, I was going to use some of my wooden

blocks to make the walls of the maze. What do you think?"

"I think that's a great idea!" I said. "You always have such good ideas."

"Here, hold Cheesy," Robbie said, handing me his mouse. "I want to try something."

I took Cheesy and held him tightly in my hands so he couldn't escape.

"I could put this block here . . . and this block here . . . ," Robbie said as he began to build the maze.

I held Cheesy up to my face. "What do you say, little guy? Do you have any good ideas for my experiment?"

"*Squeak . . . squeak . . .*"

"Sorry, I don't speak mouse language. Do you speak mouse language, Robbie?"

"Very funny," said Robbie as he continued putting the blocks into place.

"Hey, it was worth a try!" I said, laughing.

"Follow me," Robbie said.

"Where are we going?"

"Downstairs."

"But I thought you said you were going to help me think of an experiment."

"Don't worry, Freddy. I will. Right now I

want to go get some food that I think Cheesy will like, so that we can do a test run."

Robbie grabbed Cheesy from me, and we ran down the stairs and into the kitchen.

Robbie opened the refrigerator. "Let's see.... What looks good to you, little guy?" he said to Cheesy.

"*Squeak . . . squeak.*"

"Cheese. That's a good idea," said Robbie. "What else?"

"*Squeak . . . squeak.*"

"Oh, bread. Okay."

"Hey, wait a minute. I thought you said you didn't speak mouse language," I said.

Robbie laughed. "I'm joking. I just happen to know what Cheesy likes to eat."

"Everyone knows that mice like cheese," I said.

"But Cheesy likes this bread even better than cheese," Robbie said as he reached for a package of bread in the back of the refrigerator.

"I guess that makes sense," I said. "I remember Mrs. Wushy read us that story about a mouse who comes out at night looking for the crumbs the people dropped all around the house."

"Freddy, do me a favor," said Robbie. "Open the bag. I don't want Cheesy to escape."

"Sure," I said.

I opened the bag and pulled out a piece of bread. "Eeeeewwwww," I said, dropping the slice of bread onto the counter.

"What?" Robbie asked.

"Look at it! It's got fuzzy green stuff all over it!" I said.

"So?"

"So that's disgusting!"

"It's just mold," Robbie said. "If food sits around for too long, bacteria start to grow on it. That's what mold is—bacteria."

"Thanks for the explanation, Einstein. Now I think it's even more disgusting."

"Oh, don't be such a wimp, Freddy. I think mold is kind of cool."

"Of course you do," I said.

"No, really. It is. Did you know that it comes in different colors?"

"Like what?"

"Green, brown, white," Robbie said.

Cheesy squeaked.

"Yes, I know. White, just like you," Robbie said to Cheesy.

Then Robbie turned to me. "Hey! I just got a great idea!" he said.

"Yeah? What?"

"Why don't you grow mold for your experiment for the science fair?"

"That's funny . . . really funny."

"No. I'm serious. You could put a few different foods in plastic bags, and see how long it takes for mold to start growing on each one. You could also see if different kinds of mold grow on different foods."

I stared at Robbie for a minute. "Are you joking?"

"No! I'm totally serious! I think it would be a great experiment," said Robbie.

"There's only one problem," I said.

"What's that?" asked Robbie.

"Well, you know my mom is such a neat

freak. She would never let me have mold in the house."

"She doesn't have to know until you're done with the experiment."

"What do you mean?" I asked.

"You could put the food in bags here at my house and sneak it back into your house in your backpack. Then, when you're upstairs in your room, just hide the bags in your closet behind some toys. You can check on them every day for a few weeks. Your mom will never know they are there."

"I think I'm beginning to like this idea," I said.

"Kids will think it's really cool," said Robbie. "And who knows? Maybe you'll win first prize!"

"There's only one other problem."

"What now?" Robbie sighed.

"My mom will want to know what my experiment is going to be."

"Just tell her that you're doing something with me," Robbie said. "You already told her that I was going to help you."

"You're so smart! And a great friend," I said to Robbie.

"Hey, what are friends for?" Robbie said with a smile.

"*Squeak! Squeak!*" Cheesy squeaked.

CHAPTER 6

Shhhhhh . . . Don't Tell!

As soon as I got home from Robbie's house, I went straight to my room to hide the bags of food.

"Freddy, is that you?" my mom called from the kitchen.

"Yeah, Mom."

"I had some laundry I wanted you to carry up to your room."

"I'll be right down to get it. I just have to go to the bathroom."

I didn't have a lot of time. I had to hide the stuff quickly, before anyone came upstairs. I threw open my closet door and pushed aside my blow-up shark from the carnival and boxes of baseball cards. My suitcase was standing in the back of my closet.

"Perfect," I whispered to myself. We weren't going on a trip anytime soon, so my mom won't be touching that. I could hide the bags of food behind the suitcase, and she'd never see them.

I was so busy hiding the bags that I didn't hear Suzie come in. She bent down beside me and whispered in my ear, "What are you doing?"

I was so startled that I jumped about three feet into the air. "AAAAHHHHHH!"

"You told Mom that you were going to the bathroom. This doesn't look like the bathroom to me."

"Get out! Get out!" I yelled. "This is my room. No one invited you in here!"

"Well, actually Mom did," Suzie said. "She told me to bring these clothes to you."

"Just put them on my bed and get out!"

"Not until you tell me what you're doing," Suzie said. "You're trying to hide something, and I want to know what it is."

"No, I'm not. I'm looking for a baseball card."

"Liar! Your baseball card box isn't even open."

"It's none of your beeswax!" I yelled. "Now leave."

"Tell me what you just hid behind your suitcase."

"What are you talking about?" I asked.

"When I walked in, you were hiding something behind your suitcase."

"No, I wasn't."

"Come on," said Suzie. "You're up to something. Now just tell me what it is."

I was not going to win this one. She was

not going to leave my room until I told her. "Promise you won't tell Mom and Dad."

"What's it worth to you?" she asked, holding up her pinkie for a pinkie swear.

"I don't know."

"I get to choose dessert for a week," Suzie said.

"A week? You're kidding, right?"

"Do I look like I'm kidding?"

We get to take turns picking dessert each night. I usually choose ice cream, but Suzie usually picks cookies. I didn't know if I could go a whole week without ice cream.

"How about three days?" I said.

"It's a week or nothing. I don't have all day, Freddy. Do we have a deal or not?" Suzie asked, shoving her pinkie into my face.

I really didn't have a choice. If I didn't take the deal, then she would tell my mom, and I wouldn't get to do my cool experiment. "Fine. Deal," I said as we locked pinkies.

"Now, tell me what you're hiding behind your suitcase."

"Bags of food," I said.

"Bags of food? You're not allowed to have food in your room," Suzie said.

"Duh! Don't you think I know that?"

"If you're that hungry, why don't you just

ask Mom for something to eat? Or is it for a midnight snack?"

"I'm not going to eat the food," I said.

"You're not? Isn't that what most people do with food—eat it?" Suzie asked.

"I'm using it for my experiment for the science fair."

"An experiment? What kind of experiment?" Suzie asked.

"I'm going to see how long it takes for mold to grow on it," I said.

"Mold! EEEWWW! That's disgusting!" said Suzie. "Mom hates mold. She is totally grossed out by it."

"I know. That's why I have to hide it from her. If I told her I wanted to grow mold for an experiment, then she wouldn't let me."

"You've got that right."

"So, now that we have a deal, you're not going to tell her it's in my closet, right?" I asked. "Robbie said I have to leave it in there for at least two weeks."

"Two weeks? That's a long time to hide something from Mom," Suzie said.

"I know, but if it works, it's going to be the best experiment ever!" I said.

CHAPTER 7

Gone!

I kept the food hidden in my closet, and every day I checked each bag to see if anything was growing inside. At the beginning, I thought the experiment wasn't going to work, because for the first four days nothing happened. Then, on the fifth day, the foods started to grow all kinds of cool mold. Green fuzzy stuff, white bunches that looked like cotton, black goo. It was awesome! Robbie was right. This was a great experiment.

My mom and dad thought I was doing an experiment with Robbie, so some days I went over to Robbie's house after school and told them that we were working on our experiment.

One day, when almost two weeks had gone by, my mom picked me up at Robbie's house after we had been working on our experiment. At least, that's what my mom thought we were doing. When I got into the car, I was carrying a big display board that was folded up.

"So, how is your experiment coming along?" my mom asked.

"Great! Just great!" I said.

"I can't wait to see it!" my mom said.

"Well, you'll get to see it soon!" I said, smiling to myself.

"Maybe I could just get a sneak peek," she said.

"Sorry. You'll have to wait until the science fair tomorrow. I want to do this without your help."

We pulled into our driveway, and I jumped out of the car and ran upstairs to my room. I had to put all the stuff on my display board that night.

I flung open my closet door, got down on my hands and knees, and reached behind my suitcase to grab the bags of moldy food. All I felt was the carpet.

I moved my hand slowly back and forth across the ground. "I know I put the bags back right here yesterday," I thought.

I grabbed the suitcase and threw it out into my room.

Then I looked back at the spot where the bags should have been, but all I saw was a big empty space.

"No! No! NO!!!" I yelled.

Suzie stuck her head into my room. "What's your problem, Shark Breath?"

I ran over to her. "Where are my bags of food?" I yelled in her face.

"What are you talking about?" Suzie said.

"The bags of food for my experiment. They aren't there. What did you do with them?"

"Why would I want bags of moldy food? I didn't do anything with them."

Just then my mom walked into the room. "What is all the yelling about?" she asked.

Suzie looked at me, and I looked at Suzie.

"Nothing," Suzie said.

"Yeah. Nothing," I said.

"Well, I thought I heard you yelling something about food," my mom said, "and that reminds me, Freddy. Today when I came to get your suitcase for your sleepover at Papa and Grammy's house this weekend, I found some bags of moldy food on the floor of your closet."

I gulped. My eyes got wide.

"How many times have I told you that you may not bring food into your room?"

I got a sinking feeling in my stomach.

"I have no idea how long that food has been sitting in your room. It was covered in mold. It was the most disgusting thing I have ever seen!" my mom said.

"What did you do with it?" I asked.

"What did I do with it? What do you *think* I did with it? I threw it in the trash."

"NOOOOOOOOOO!!!!" I screamed. I threw myself onto my bed and started to cry.

"Freddy," said my mom, "what is the matter with you?"

"Now it's ruined! It's all ruined!" I sobbed.

"What's ruined?" asked my mom.

"My . . . my . . . my experiment!"

"Your experiment? What are you talking about? I thought you were doing an experiment with Robbie."

"Robbie's idea . . . mold . . . food . . . ," I wailed.

"Freddy, you need to stop crying. I can't understand a thing you're saying," said my mom. "Why don't you sit up and take a few deep breaths?"

I slowly sat up and tried to gulp some air.

"There," said my mom. "That's better. Now, why don't you start from the beginning?"

"Well . . . I couldn't think of a good
experiment for the science fair," I said, sniffling,
"but one day when I was at Robbie's house, we
found mold on some bread in his refrigerator."

"Ewwww. Gross," Suzie said.

My mom made a face.

I blew my nose loudly into a Kleenex. "Anyway, that gave Robbie a good idea. He said that I should see how long it took for mold to grow on different foods. I really liked that idea, but I knew you would never let me have moldy food in the house, so I hid it in my closet," I said, still choking back sobs.

"Oh, Freddy," my mom said, patting my back.

"So the food you threw out today was actually my experiment for the science fair!" I sobbed.

"Wait!" Suzie said. "I have an idea."

I looked up at her.

"Why don't you just get it out of the trash can?"

I grabbed my mom's hand. "Come on, Mom! Let's go get it out of the trash."

My mom didn't move.

I yanked on her harder. "Come on!"

"I'm sorry, Freddy," my mom said, "but today was trash day. Those bags have been taken to the dump."

I fell to the floor and started hitting the ground with my fists. "NO! NO! NO!" I screamed.

"Freddy, stop that this instant!" my mom said as she picked me up off the floor. "You're acting like a baby."

"But you threw out my experiment!" I wailed. "The science fair is tomorrow, and now I don't have a project for it!"

"I'm sorry I accidentally threw out your experiment, but this wouldn't have happened if you hadn't lied to me."

I sniffled and wiped my nose on my sleeve. "So what am I going to do?" I asked.

"I have another idea," said Suzie. "You could just draw pictures of what the food looked like with the mold growing on it."

"But that's not as cool as having the real moldy food hanging on my display board," I said.

"I don't think you have a choice," said my mom. "It's too late to do another experiment."

I hung my head.

"I just hope you learned your lesson, Freddy," my mom said.

I nodded. "Mom?"

"What?"

"I think I might need your help after all."

CHAPTER 8

And the Winner Is . . .

Both my mom and Suzie helped me finish my display board. The next night we went to the science fair. All my friends were there with their projects.

Chloe's board was decorated with pink and purple ribbons, and if you looked at her project, she would paint your fingernails.

"Don't go near Chloe's spot unless you want pink fingernails," Jessie said, holding up her hands.

"I thought you didn't like pink," I said.

"I don't," said Jessie. "She grabbed me before I could get away!"

We both laughed.

"Hey, you guys! Come over here," yelled Max.

Jessie and I tried to ignore him, but he called again. "Jessie, Freddy, come over here!"

"I really don't want to see cut-up worms," I said to Jessie.

"Me, either," Jessie said. She stuck her tongue out. "It's so gross."

We walked slowly over to Max's spot.

"Come closer, guys, so you can get a really good look," said Max.

Max's board was actually pretty cool. He had glued on some photos of the worms cut in half and then pictures of them whole again.

"See this here?" he asked, pointing to one of the pictures. "I cut this guy in half, and

then a little while later he looked like this." He pointed to a picture of a whole worm.

"Wow! I didn't know that worms could do that," I said.

Max had a jar of live worms sitting on the

table in front of him. "Do you want to hold one, Freddy?" he asked.

I took a few steps back.

"Are you afraid of a little old worm?" Max asked, dangling it in my face.

"Uh . . . no," I said. "I just have to go over to see Jessie's project now." I grabbed Jessie's arm and yanked her away before Max could drop the worm down my shirt.

"Where's your project, Jessie?" I asked.

"It's over here. Follow me."

I followed Jessie to her spot. "Your board is so cool," I said. It was covered in green plants cut out of paper.

"Thank you," said Jessie. "I decorated it myself."

She had two live plants sitting in front of her board. One was really green and had big jalapeños growing on it, and the other one was brown and droopy.

Jessie pointed to the brown one. "I left that one in the closet for two weeks. It didn't get any sunlight," she said.

"It looks dead," I said.

"It is," said Jessie. "I guess this proves that jalapeño plants really do need sunlight to grow. My *abuela* was right."

"Let's go see Robbie's project," I said. "I think you're really going to like it."

We walked over to Robbie's spot. His display board was covered in charts and graphs and photos of his experiment. The maze he had built for Cheesy was sitting on the table in front of him, and he was holding Cheesy in his hands.

"Wow!" said Jessie. "This is so cool, Robbie. Did you build this maze all by yourself?"

"Yep," Robbie said, smiling.

"What was Cheesy's favorite thing to run through the maze for?" Jessie asked.

"Chocolate-chip cookies," said Robbie.

We all laughed.

"*I* would run through a maze for chocolate-chip cookies," Jessie said.

"Me, too!" I said.

"Hey, Freddy," said Robbie, "I haven't seen your project yet. Will you show it to me?"

"Well . . . umm . . ."

"What's the matter?" Robbie asked. "I thought you loved the mold idea."

"I did. I mean, I do. It's just that I had a little accident."

"What kind of accident?" asked Robbie.

"My mom threw out my experiment."

"Why would she do that?" Jessie asked.

"She didn't do it on purpose. I had it hiding in my closet, and she thought it was trash, so she threw it out."

"Bummer," said Jessie. "So what did you do?"

"Come over, and I'll show you."

Jessie and Robbie followed me over to my spot. Robbie carried Cheesy in his pocket. "I had to draw pictures of what the moldy food looked like," I said, pointing to my display board.

"It still looks good," said Jessie.

"It would have been so much cooler to have the real bags of moldy food hanging on my board. There's no way I'll win first prize now."

Just as I said that, Mr. Pendergast, the principal, turned on his microphone.

"There are some amazing projects here tonight," he said. "You are all wonderful scientists. But now it is time for me to give out the prize for the best experiment."

"I hope I win! I hope I win!" Chloe squealed as she waved her pink fingernails in the air.

"The winner of this year's science fair is . . ."

I held my breath.

"Robbie Jackson."

"That's me! That's me!" Robbie yelled.

Everyone started clapping.

When he walked up to get his prize, all the noise must have scared Cheesy, because he jumped out of Robbie's pocket and ran right toward Chloe.

"EEEEEEEEEK!!!! EEEEEEEEEK!!!!! A mouse! A mouse!" she screamed, and she jumped up onto her display table.

Robbie dove toward Cheesy and chased him through the maze of tables.

I ran to Robbie's display and grabbed one of the chocolate-chip cookies he had used for his experiment. I broke it into pieces and threw it onto the floor.

"Freddy, what are you doing?" asked my mom. "You're making a mess."

"You'll see," I said, and smiled.

Cheesy stopped running, turned around, and headed right for one of the cookie crumbs.

As he nibbled on it, Robbie caught him in his hands.

"Thanks, Freddy," Robbie said. "You're a genius."

"I just figured all these tables were like a big maze," I said.

"You're lucky Freddy thought of that," Robbie said to Cheesy, "or else I might have lost you. I hope you learned your lesson, little guy."

"I think we both learned a lesson," I said. "Right, Cheesy?"

"Squeak! Squeak!"

DEAR READER,

I am a kindergarten and first-grade teacher. Every year my school has a science fair. I love science, and it's always exciting to see the amazing projects the students do.

One year, a third-grade student did an experiment with mice, just like Robbie. She brought the mice to school the night of the science fair, and someone accidentally unlocked the cage. The mice jumped out and started running all over the cafeteria! People were screaming, and one teacher even jumped up onto a table because she was so afraid of mice. Finally, the girl caught her mice, but it was one of the craziest science fairs ever!

I hope you have as much fun reading *Science Fair Flop* as I had writing it.

HAPPY READING!

Abby Klein

Freddy's Fun Pages

FREDDY'S SHARK JOURNAL

STUDYING SHARKS

Check out these three ways that scientists can study sharks in the ocean.

Scientists can tag sharks. First they catch the shark, and then they stick a tag into one of its fins. If the tag is electronic, then it gives off a sound that can be detected by equipment the scientists have on their boat. This way they can follow the movement of the shark.

Scientists can put on diving gear and get into a big cage that is lowered into the ocean from a boat. People on the boat throw dead fish into the water to attract the sharks. The divers in the cage wait for the sharks to swim close, and then they can take pictures of them with underwater cameras.

 Scientists can observe sharks up close by wearing a special diving suit called a chain-mail suit. It is made of lots of small metal hooks that the sharks cannot bite through. If the scientists wear these suits, then they can get close enough to pet the shark!

TRY YOUR OWN EXPERIMENT!

These three experiments are some of Freddy's favorites. Maybe you'd like to try one for your next science fair!

Experiment #1

How permanent are permanent markers?

YOU WILL NEED:

a permanent marker   alcohol

four cloths   vinegar

water

1. Draw three lines about six inches apart from each other with the permanent marker on a piece of cloth.

2. Pour some water on the first line and rub it with another cloth. Did the line disappear?

3. Pour some alcohol on the second line and rub it with another cloth. Did the line disappear?

4. Pour some vinegar on the third line and rub it with another cloth. Did the line disappear?

Which of the liquids (if any) made the marker line disappear? You can also test different brands of permanent markers to see if you get different results.

Experiment #2

Do different brands of microwave popcorn leave different amounts of unpopped kernels?

YOU WILL NEED:

a microwave

three brands of microwave popcorn

three bowls

paper and a pencil

1. With an adult's help, pop one bag of brand A microwave popcorn. When the bag is cool enough to open, dump the contents into a bowl. Separate the unpopped kernels from the rest of the popcorn.

Count the kernels and write down the number on a sheet of paper.

2. Do the same thing with one bag of brand B popcorn and record the number of unpopped kernels.

3. Do the same thing with one bag of brand C popcorn and record the number of unpopped kernels.

Did all three brands leave the same number of kernels unpopped, or did any of the brands leave fewer unpopped kernels than the others?

Which one would you rather buy?

Experiment #3

Do all brands of bubble gum make the same size bubble?

YOU WILL NEED:

a few different brands
  of bubble gum

a ruler

a pencil and some
  paper

1. Unwrap a piece of bubble gum. Chew it until it is soft enough to blow a bubble. Blow a bubble and have your mom or dad measure it (before it pops!) using the ruler. Blow and measure five bubbles with this piece of gum. Don't forget to record the size of your bubbles on a piece of paper.

2. Spit out your first piece of gum and put a different brand of bubble gum into your mouth. Repeat the steps from above with this piece of gum.

3. Spit out your second piece of gum and put the third brand of bubble gum into your mouth. Repeat the steps with this piece of gum.

Did you blow bigger bubbles with one brand than with the others? You can also test whether some brands stick to your face more than others when the bubbles pop!

Don't miss any of Freddy's funny adventures!